THE GHOST
OF THE
COG-WHEEL RAILWAY

John Szemerey

AUSTIN MACAULEY PUBLISHERS™

LONDON • CAMBRIDGE • NEW YORK • SHARJAH

Copyright © John Szemerey (2020)

A CIP catalogue record for this title is available from the British Library.

ISBN   9781528948609   (Paperback)
ISBN   9781528948616   (Hardback)
ISBN   9781528972338   (ePub e-book)

www.austinmacauley.com

First Published (2020)
Austin Macauley Publishers Ltd
25 Canada Square
Canary Wharf
London
E14 5LQ

This book is dedicated to my children, Samantha and Mark, who have been begging me to write this story since I first told it to them when on a family holiday in Hungary.

Foreword

This story takes place in Budapest, the capital of Hungary. Hungary is a small country in the centre of Europe.

Buda and Pest are parts of Budapest. One of Europe's biggest rivers, the Danube, runs through Budapest. Buda is on one side of the river, and Pest is on the other side. Buda is hilly, while Pest is flat.

One of the hills of Buda is rather steep, which would make it difficult for a normal railway to go up or down the hill without slipping. In cold, icy weather, a normal railway would not be able to get a grip on the rails. If it tried, there would be a great danger that the wheels would just spin and the train would not move, or if it managed to get up part of the way, it would slip and slide down to the bottom again.

So the Hungarians have built a special railway that can climb hills. It has a central rail with strong horizontal metal blades a few inches from each other, all the way from the terminus at the bottom of the hill to the end station at the top.

Underneath the specially designed trains are wheels with strong cogs that grip the blades on the central rail to go safely up and down the hill. The engine of each train turns the cogwheels under each carriage, and the cogs firmly grip the blades of the central rail. The cogwheels turn to make the train go up or down the hill. With cogs on each carriage firmly gripping the central rail, there is no possibility of the train slipping or sliding, even in cold, icy weather.

It is this railway that Zoltán has always wanted to drive.

Chapter 1

Zoltán was on his way up to Heaven. His life had been full and active, and yesterday afternoon and evening, his family and friends had arranged a splendid 80th birthday party for him. It had been a lovely party. Over 50 relatives and friends had come to celebrate him. The food and drink was delicious. Daughters, cousins, nieces had all cooked or brought his favourite dishes and mixed his favourite drinks – so of course he ate and drank from everything. And it was all yummy!

Zoltán is a friendly chap, so he had made a point of going round to talk to everyone. At the end, he was very tired. When the guests had all gone, he settled down in his favourite armchair and fell asleep, with a contented smile over his face. He dreamt of the party. He dreamt of his family. He dreamt of his friends and of his long life working for the railways – the last 20 years of which he had been an engine driver.

Gradually, his dreams became blurred and faint. His breathing slowed, and then stopped. He was dead.

The angels who decide where to send dead persons – to Heaven or to Hell – had no doubt with Zoltán. He had been a good man, loved by his children and grandchildren. He was always ready to help a friend or colleague in trouble. He had been one of the best engine drivers on the Hungarian railways. He was never late for work. He always had a cheerful word for his workmates. So he was sent up to Heaven.

Passing through the clouds, he eventually spotted a beautiful city. In front, there was an enormous decorative gate through which everyone had to go. Just outside, an old bearded man sat at a large desk. He was St Peter, who decided who could get into Heaven and who could not. Beside him was a large lever, which operated the gates.

Zoltán had to join a queue of people who had died recently to be checked by St Peter on their qualifications for Heaven. After half an hour, it was his turn.

"Welcome, Zoltán!" said the beaming saint. "You've been a good man. You deserve to be with us in Heaven.

"You also deserve a special wish, if there is anything you want."

"Thank you, sir," said the modest engine driver. "In fact, I have all I want, so there is no need to ask you for anything."

Suddenly he remembered. All his life he had wanted to drive the cogwheel railway up and down the Buda hills. He knew it was too late for that, but he would mention it to St Peter.

"No problem!" replied the smiling saint. "We can take care of that. But remember, you are no longer a normal man. You're a spirit, what people call a ghost.

"I can arrange for you to drive the cog-wheel railway up and down the Buda hills at night, when the railway is officially closed. All the signals and points will work automatically, so all you need to do is to drive. People will see the train, but no one will see you, as you are a ghost.

"You can start tonight. At midnight."

"Oh thank you, sir! Thank you! Thank you!" stuttered the delighted Zoltán.

"Be at the gates by quarter to midnight," said St Peter.

"I'll be there, sir!" replied the happy Zoltán. "I'll be there!"

And so he was. Well before 11.45, he was at the Pearly Gates, looking forward to the drive of his life.

Chapter 2

The doors of the railway shed opened all by themselves. The lights of the train came on, and the motor started all by itself. Zoltán, to his surprise, was at the controls in the driver's cabin at the front of the train.

"Now it is up to you," whispered a soft voice in his ear.

Ding, ding! he thumped on the train's bell, and the train was off. He slowly edged the control lever forward, and the train emerged from its shed. It slowly rolled round to the station and stopped at its usual platform.

It's working! thought Zoltán. *It's working! I'm driving the cogwheel railway!*

He waited a couple of minutes so passengers – if there were any – could get on or off. Then he rang the bell to signal that the train was leaving, and he moved the driving lever forward.

Ding, ding! said the front carriage, and the train started its climb uphill, its cogwheels engaging the metal teeth of the special central rails. And, visible only to ghosts and angels, there was a beaming Zoltán at the controls, looking earnestly through the front window.

This was a special train. The mountain railway was the only one of its kind in Hungary, if not in the world. It climbed up and down a steep hill, the Buda Hill, on the West side of Budapest, capital of Hungary. It needed cogwheels to get a grip on the rails so it could climb up, and it needed cogwheels to hold itself steady as it came down.

A normal train would never have climbed that hill. Nor would it have been able to go down without sliding out of control. In winter, when the rails were covered with snow and ice, it would not have been able to start at all. But the cogwheel railway could safely go up and down the steep hill in all conditions, in all weather.

Ding, ding! sounded the train as it came to the first stop up the hill. Zoltán slowed the train down and stopped it alongside the empty platform. He allowed the regulation couple of minutes for passengers to get on and off. Then he looked in the driver's mirror. No doors open along the platform, so he could go.

Ding, ding! And off went the train.

The track was surrounded by trees and the gardens of elegant villas. In places it was like driving through an avenue of overarching trees. Then came the next garden, at the end of which was a smart villa, and so on.

Some villas still had lights on, as not everyone goes to bed before midnight.

No one noticed the train going uphill, except Arthur, Dr Práger's very alert Bernese mountain dog. Arthur picked up his ears. He heard a strange noise, which he normally never heard at night. Was something wrong? "Woof!" he barked with a deep loud voice. "Woof, woof!"

And as often happens when a dog starts to bark, the other dogs in the neighbourhood also started to bark, making one hell of a noise. Lights went on in several houses. But those that thought they heard something could not believe their ears. *What?* they thought, *A train going uphill at this time of night? Can't be. Or perhaps it is something special. Perhaps taking supplies up the line, for repairs. Or testing something new on the railway.*

"Woof, woof!" continued Arthur. "Woof, woof, woof!"

"Ooooou! Yap, yap, yap!" echoed the dogs in nearby houses.

Of course, Zoltán heard the noise in the train's driving cab. He knew all the dogs – as ghosts do – so he smiled and called out in a friendly voice, "Arthur! It's only me!" followed by a chuckle.

Arthur gave a surprised squeak and two more woofs for good measure. Then he stopped barking. And all the dogs in the neighbourhood stopped barking too.

The cats in the neighbourhood also heard the train and the dogs. Their hearing is better than that of dogs, and by nature, they are very alert at night. So Shadow, the senior cat of the neighbourhood – a beautiful long-haired black cat –called a meeting of his cat lieutenants to decide what to do.

"We can't let the dogs make a better impression on our masters than us," said Shadow to the meeting. "So let us all rush onto the train one day, and we could meow together in unison. That would be heard by everyone, and it would make a good news story in the newspapers."

The cats decided on a day early the following week. Before they went home, Shadow called out if there were any strays at the meeting. Three cats stood up on their hind feet and gave a short meow.

"So you are strays? You have no regular home?" asked Shadow.

"Meow!" replied each of the three cats, shaking their heads.

"Good," said Shadow. "Then be sure to be with us next Tuesday when we jump onto the cog-wheel train. Then remain on the train when the rest of us get off. A man will come from the Cat Society. He will catch you and take you back to the Society's house. They always have people looking for nice cats, and within days you will have found homes."

"Any other urgent business?"

None of the cats had any other urgent matter to discuss, so the meeting closed and they all went home.

With the dogs stopping to bark and no one being aware of the cats' plans, no one called the police or the railway company to complain about the cogwheel railway going up and down hill during the night. No one worried. No one complained.

The railway's lights lit up the tracks in front of the train and the trees on either side. The trees in silhouette were very beautiful, outlined against the deep blue of the sky. Others looked like scarecrows. As the train passed villas with different sorts of gardens, Zoltán wondered about the people who lived there.

Ding, ding! The train was approaching the next stop. Zoltán slid the control lever round towards him, and the train stopped perfectly, alongside the platform. The lights were still on – they stayed on all night – so anyone wanting to get on or off the train could do so safely.

Zoltán looked round. It was a beautiful night.

There was a little moonlight, so he could see quite a bit of the nightscape. Stars twinkled in the sky.

But it was time to go. He must not keep his passengers waiting. He looked in the driver's mirror. All clear. So he thumped on the bell. Ding, ding! And off went the train, continuing on its way uphill.

And so it went, all the way up the Buda Hill. Zoltán kept the train waiting several minutes at the end station on top of the hill, as this allowed drivers to relax and have a little rest. He checked everything was in order and switched off in the driver's cab. Then he got out and walked along the platform to the other end of the train.

He climbed into the driver's cab at that end. He put the key into the motor and turned it on. He checked the lights were on. The train was ready to leave.

Ding, ding! and off went the train. It wound its way down the hill, the cogs gripping the rails firmly so the train would not run out of control. Zoltán stopped the train at every stop, allowing time for passengers to get on and off. Then ding, ding! and the train continued on its way.

Of course there were no passengers, as the railway was closed for the night.

Finally, the train drew into the terminus at the bottom of the hill. Zoltán knew it was time to put it away for the night. So he walked round to the other end of the train. He got into the driver's cab, checked that the points had been changed and the rails were pointing towards the railway shed.

Then ding, ding! and the train slowly moved out. The great doors of the engine shed opened, and the train slid into its usual place between the other two cogwheel trains that operated on the line during the day.

Zoltán checked that everything was switched off. He climbed down out of the cab. Suddenly he felt himself floating – floating up through the roof and then up into the sky and into Heaven.

A smiling St Peter was waiting for him at the gates. "Well, Zoltán, how was it?"

"Oh, marvellous, sir! It was marvellous! Thank you, thank you!"

"Well, as this was your wish on entering Heaven," said St Peter, "you can drive the cog-wheel railway every night. Just be at the Pearly Gates at quarter to midnight.

"But," he added, "don't always expect it to be as easy and trouble-free as tonight."

Chapter 3

Zoltán was as good as his word. Day after day he came along to the Pearly Gates a quarter of an hour before midnight. As if by magic, he was transported to the shed where the cogwheel railways were locked up for the night. The lights went on. The engine of the train in the middle started up as Zoltán climbed into the driver's cab. He took hold of the controls and gently pushed the driving lever round to the right. The shed doors opened. The train's engine whirred, and the cogwheel railway edged its way forward, round to the terminal station at the bottom of the Buda Hills.

Then ding! ding! and the train was off on its journey uphill, with a happy Zoltán at the controls.

On the third night that Zoltán drove the train, Arthur still barked once or twice, people living nearby started making comments to their neighbours, asking each other what was going on. One of them, an important lawyer, phoned the police to complain.

"Officer," he said, "Can you find out what's going on? I hope it is not hooligans playing with the railway. That could be dangerous. Or are the railway people doing something special when there is no one around?"

"I don't know, sir," replied a policeman. "We have no news of any night-time works on the railway. But I will be happy to check."

"In any case," continued the lawyer, "the noise is a nuisance. Night after night the train goes up and down the Buda Hill, ringing its bell as it arrives at every stop and when it leaves, and all the local dogs start to bark.

"It's a damned nuisance! Many of us cannot sleep. Can you get the railway people to lock their trains up at night, so people living near the mountain railway are not woken up or kept awake by a train going up and down hill?"

The police sent a patrol car to the lawyer's villa. Two policemen got out and checked with the lawyer. He pointed out that the mountain railway went by the end of his garden, and complained that the noise of a railway rattling its way up and down hill some time after midnight shattered the calm and quiet of the night.

"Just leave it to us, sir!" said the older policeman, a sergeant, giving a knowing smile.

Then he had an idea. "Has the train gone by yet, tonight?" he asked.

"Yes," replied the lawyer, "that's why I called you. But it has not come down yet. It should be passing fairly soon."

As he said that, a faint metallic clattering could be heard approaching.

"Come, Gyula!" the sergeant called to his colleague. He ran towards a path that led to the nearest stop of the mountain railway. His colleague followed.

By the time they got to the stop, the cogwheel railway was already there, waiting for passengers who wanted to get on or off. Of course, there were no passengers, but Zoltán was well trained to allow time at every stop and station for anyone who wished to get on or off.

The two policemen ran alongside the train to the driver's cab at the front. They wanted to see who was driving the train and why.

When they got to the front of the train, they had a shock. The driver's cab was empty! The engine driver was nowhere to be seen! He must have heard them coming and was hiding somewhere, thought the policemen. So they searched the train.

Zoltán, of course, was driving the train, and he was there in the driver's cab. But he was invisible to normal living people. He saw the searching policemen, but he had to respect the timetable. So he rang the train's bell as a warning, ding! ding! After a few seconds, which should have been enough for the policemen to get off, he closed the doors, edged the driving lever forward and the train moved off.

The elder policeman was on the platform, so he ran to the front of the train to see who was driving. He still could not see Zoltán, so he thought that whoever was driving had ducked to the floor so he or she could not be seen.

Meanwhile the younger policeman, Gyula, was searching the carriages when the doors locked and the train started to move. He had jumped on when the train was at the stop.

"Stop!" shouted the sergeant. "Stop!" shouted Gyula, gesticulating wildly in the third carriage.

But Zoltán did not hear. He just happily drove the train downhill, away from the stop.

"Get off!" the sergeant shouted to his colleague.

"I can't!" replied Gyula. "The doors are locked!"

So he went up the train, from carriage to carriage until he reached the front carriage. But the driver's cab is separate from the rest of the carriage, and the connecting door was locked. He banged on the door to get the driver to open it, but nothing happened. He pulled and pushed at the door handle, but the door would not budge.

He then grabbed the handle with both hands and put his feet against the door to give more force to his pull. Suddenly – Crash! – the door handle broke off, and poor Gyula went flying half way down the carriage. But the door remained locked.

Gyula noticed that the train was slowing down. Ding! ding! went the train's bell as it drew up at the next stop. Gyula jumped to his feet and dashed to the nearest door. It opened without trouble, and Gyula leapt out.

"I know you're there!" he shouted towards the driver's cab. "You can't get away now!"

He tore open the door of the driver's cab – but it was empty. No one to be seen.

Unknown to him, Zoltán was still there at the controls. But he could not be seen, as he was a spirit.

Zoltán was rather enjoying the antics of the policeman. He smiled contentedly as Gyula searched every inch of the driver's cab.

Then as the policeman climbed out of the driver's cab, Zoltán sounded the train's bell. He pulled the cab door shut and started the train again on its downhill journey.

"Stop!" screamed the astonished Gyula. He jumped up and down to see into the driver's cab, but could see no one. He tried to open the cab door again, but he could not. It locked automatically before the train could move. He tried to jump into the passing carriages, but their doors were also locked.

So he found himself all alone on the platform, with the cogwheel railway rattling its way downhill.

It did not occur to the elder policeman that Gyula would get out of the mountain railway at the next stop, so he drove down to the terminus at the bottom of the hill, to be there when the railway arrived.

Poor Gyula did not have his police radio with him, and he could not contact his colleague or the police station. So he had to walk all the way down hill and into town. Finally, 45 minutes later in town, he was able to wave down a passing police car, to whose occupants he recounted what had happened that night, as they drove him back to the police station.

The sergeant had meanwhile driven the patrol car to the railway terminus, and he waited for the train to appear.

Sure enough, after ten minutes, he heard the clattering of an approaching railway. It was the cogwheel train that he had seen up on the hill. He hid so the driver would not see him, and he waited to pounce on the driver the moment he got off the train.

But no one got off the train! He saw the door of the driver's cab open, so he dashed to grab whoever came out. But no one did. And the cab door slammed shut. He ran over to it, but could not open it. It was locked, as if by magic. Standing on his toes, he looked into the cab, but there was no one to be seen.

Meanwhile, Zoltán got out and watched the policeman hurry along the platform beside the train, looking thoroughly into every carriage. He walked down to the other end of the train, passing within inches of the bewildered policeman, and opened the door of the driver's cab. He got in and gave a little chuckle. He sounded the train's bell, ding! ding! and slowly the train rolled round to its place in the railway shed.

The policeman could hardly believe his eyes. He did not dare to follow the train into its shed, as he was on his own and felt it could be dangerous to do so.

"Something funny is going on!" he muttered to himself. And he determined to discover what it was. But for that night he had had enough. So he drove back to the police station, arriving just minutes before his colleague, Gyula.

Chapter 4

The police were very angry. They were certain that someone was making fun of them by driving the cogwheel railway at night when it was supposed to be resting, locked away in its shed. So they decided to lay a trap, to catch the person responsible.

But no one was aware that it was Tuesday night when Shadow and the local cats had decided to ride on the ghost train.

That night, all the local policemen were on duty. A team of three, headed by the sergeant, went over to the terminal station at the bottom end of the line. They hid so no one could see them, and they waited.

The other policemen from that district waited in the police station, with a fleet of police cars and police buses, so they could go anywhere they were needed.

Sure enough, just after midnight the doors of the railway shed opened, and out came the cogwheel train. It slowly rolled over to its usual platform in the station. Zoltán got out and went to the driving cab at the other end of the train.

The train waited a few minutes, to allow time for any passengers to get on. Then Zoltán sounded the train's bell to indicate that it was about to start: ding, ding! and off went the train on its journey up the Buda hill.

"I don't know what's going on," the sergeant said to the two policemen with him. "But now we have got him! He has to go all the way to the top of the hill – and we will be waiting for him!"

He radioed the police station. "Yes? Police here," came the answer. The sergeant asked to speak to the chief inspector and reported what had happened. The cogwheel railway was on its way up the hill. So the police piled into their cars, vans and buses and dashed to the railway station at the top of the hill, where they would set a trap for the mysterious driver of the train.

They drove at high speed, but without sounding their sirens. They did not want to warn the train driver that they were coming, as he could then stop the train somewhere, get off and escape.

Meanwhile all the local cats had gathered in a large garden close to where the cogwheel railway went up and down hill. The garden was also close to where the cogwheel railway had a regular halt, where the train always stopped.

Shadow stood up on his hind feet and explained the plans to all the cats.

"The important thing," said Shadow, "is to stand up on your hind feet and grab the brass handle on the outside of all doors. Then jump up, holding the handle. Your weight will pull it down and the door will open. Then everyone can get in and settle on the comfortable seats. If you can manage it, pull the doors too, but if it is too difficult, don't worry. The train will close them automatically before it can leave the station.

"I will go into the driver's compartment, as I hear that Zoltán likes cats."

So the cats moved into position all around the station and waited for the train.

Unaware of all this, the police were preparing to catch the engine driver at the top end station of the mountain railway.

The sergeant and the two constables arrived first. The sergeant worked out a plan about where everyone should hide. As the other policemen arrived, he told them where to go, so both sides of the train were covered.

"We've got him now!" grinned the sergeant.

"He can't get away this time," he sniggered to his boss, the chief inspector.

Meanwhile, the train was grinding its way uphill, with a happy Zoltán at the controls. As the train came to a halt at the third stop a posse of some 30 cats ran onto the platform. They ran over to the nearest carriages, jumped up and grabbed the door handles, which moved down under their weight and opened the doors. The cats jumped aboard, purring happily.

Zoltán realised what was happening, so he opened the door of his driving cab, and Shadow – who had just reached the front of the train – jumped in.

Zoltán smiled broadly and called out to the long-haired black cat, "Welcome, Shadow!" and he leant down to pat him on the head.

"Meow!" replied the cat, who could see the ghost, as all animals can.

Zoltán picked him up and put him on the dashboard so he would have a good view of where they went. He then closed the doors of the train, rang the bell, Ding, ding! and off went the train towards the top of the hill.

Shadow loved this. He was being given a special viewing place to see where they went. However, he was a cat, and he was fully visible to anyone looking from outside, while Zoltán of course could not be seen.

A few minutes later, the clanking sound of the cogwheel railway could be heard, as it approached the top of the hill. And gradually its headlight could be seen, winding its way up the track.

Ding, ding! sounded the train's bell as it entered the station. Straining their eyes to see who was driving the train, the police were amazed to see a black cat at the controls, and no human driver. Then the train ground its way to a halt, within half a metre of the buffers at the end of the line.

"Now!" shouted the sergeant, jumping up from his hiding place.

Thirty-eight policemen jumped up, or jumped out from their hiding places on either side of the train, and rushed to the carriage nearest to them. They yanked the doors open and jumped in, shouting, "Come out! We know you're in there!"

As they opened each carriage door, cats jumped out, hissing and clawing towards their faces. Only Shadow stuck with Zoltán as he closed down the driver's cabin and walked to the cabin at the other end of the train.

The police rushed from carriage to carriage. They ran up to the driver's cab, and down to the other end of the train to the driver's cab for going downhill. They looked under the seats. They opened the doors leading from one carriage to the other. They climbed up on the carriage roofs. But they only found cats. Several times they nearly fell over cats jumping in and out of the train.

Gradually their faces grew longer. There was no one on the train, only cats! The mysterious driver had again got away!

The invisible Zoltán had been watching all this activity with interest. He realised that they were looking for him, but he knew they could not see him. So he was safe. He gently walked down the platform alongside the train to the driver's cab at the other end, followed by Shadow. The door opened the moment he touched the handle, and he and Shadow climbed in.

The police sergeant, who was standing not far from the end of the train, saw the door of the driver's cab open and shut, and he saw the long-haired black cat jump in.

"He is here!" he shouted, running to the driver's cab. He grabbed the door handle and tried to wrench the door open. But he could not. The door was already locked. He stood on the step by the driver's cab to see better into the cab. A well-groomed black cat was sitting at the controls. But there was no human driver there.

"I know you're in there!" he cried, hammering on the door with his fists. "Everyone over here!" he shouted to the other policemen, who came running to the driver's cab at the end of the train pointing downhill.

There were policemen all round the driver's cab. Four were even in front of it, trying to look under the train and into the driver's cab. But there was no one to be seen, apart from the black cat.

Zoltán laughed. He was amused at all this activity. But he felt that he must respect the timetable. As soon as the last policeman had got off the train and closed the carriage door he sounded the train's bell, ding, ding! and slowly the train edged its way forward, out of the station and downhill.

The policemen in front of the train jumped for their lives. The others alongside the train tried to pull open the doors. But they could not, as they were all automatically locked the moment the train started to move. They hammered with their fists on the side of the train and shouted angrily: "You can't get away with this! We'll get you!"

The train happily clattered away on the start of its downhill journey.

"What's going on, Sergeant?" demanded the chief inspector. "Can't you arrest the man who has driven this train uphill?"

"There is no one on board, sir," replied the embarrassed sergeant, "other than a handful of cats."

"No one on board? A handful of cats?" yelled the senior officer. "Do you think this train has come uphill by itself – perhaps to enjoy the night air? Or that it is being driven by cats?"

"I dunno, sir," mumbled the sergeant. "We have searched the train from end to end. And there is no one on board, apart from the cats."

"Yes, I am sure you have," growled the chief inspector. "And what are you doing now? Are you letting him get away? Or do you think he will come back uphill for you to arrest him? And send you a cat as a prize?"

"Of course not, sir. We will catch him at the other end," said the sergeant, furiously grinding his teeth.

"Everyone back in their cars and buses!" shouted the sergeant. "Down to the terminal station at the bottom! Quick! And be there before the train!"

The police scuttled back to their vehicles, and with a loud slamming of doors and noisy revving of engines the cars and buses shot off from the station, on their way downhill. This time they sounded their sirens so everything should get out of their way.

The people living in nearby houses wondered what was going on. Had they caught the fellow who was driving the train?

Chapter 5

Police cars screeched to a halt in the parking lot by the terminal station. They were followed by three police buses.

The sergeant was one of the first to arrive, and he instructed everyone where to hide. Policemen were even posted outside all the gates and entrances. *The mysterious train driver must not see them,* he thought. *Otherwise he might get away.*

Everyone waited in complete silence. The station's lights were on, but there was no one to be seen. It was eerie.

Suddenly the train's headlight could be seen, winding its way down hill. As it approached, everyone strained their eyes, to see who was driving. A black cat! All they could see was a smart long-haired black cat at the driving controls, looking calmly out of the cab.

As the train approached the station the sergeant called out, "Don't move till the train stops! Then rush to open the carriage door nearest to you. Don't worry about cats. We want the driver."

Ding, ding! sounded the train, as it entered the station. It slowed down. Then there was a screech of brakes as Zoltán stopped the train just a couple of metres from the inside end of the platform. He pressed a button to unlock the doors, so passengers could get off. But of course there were no passengers. However, most of the cats that had remained on the train jumped out. Only the three homeless strays stayed on board.

"Now! Get him!" cried the sergeant, and 38 policemen rushed to the train, snatching open the doors and jumping on to see who was there. The sergeant and Gyula dashed to the driver's cab. They pulled the door open and shouted, "Got you now! Come out and let's see who you are!"

"Meow!" called Shadow, greeting the anxious policemen.

Zoltán smiled. He was not worried, as he knew the policemen could not see or touch him, and he would not allow them to touch Shadow. He switched off the motor, turned off the lights, and checked that the brakes were properly on.

Turning to the cat, he quietly said, "Time to go home now, Shadow. Bye!" The cat stood up on his hind legs. Zoltán leant down to him, and they rubbed noses. Zoltán added, "You and your friends are always welcome on the ghost train. Just come to any of the stops along the line. There will be time for you to get on." Shadow happily jumped down from the driver's cab, called a cheerful Meow! and ran off home.

Smiling at the eager policemen, Zoltán squeezed between them as he got off, and he walked down to the other end of the train. He was able to pass between policemen getting on and off the train and searching everywhere – under the train, under the seats, in the luggage racks and even on top of the train.

The door of the cab at the other end of the train was open, as a policeman had just checked that there was no one in there. So Zoltán got on. The policeman, who had not seen Zoltán, called out, "No one here!" and he slammed the door shut.

"Thank you," said Zoltán, but the policeman did not hear through the closed door. And Zoltán got ready to drive the train round to the railway shed.

The police were mystified. They could not find anyone on the train, hard as they searched.

The chief inspector went over to the sergeant. "Well?" he asked. "Where is the driver? Or has he got away again?"

"No one could get away from that train, sir... apart from a few cats!" he replied angrily. "But there is no one to catch."

"No one to catch?" retorted the chief inspector. "Are you dumb?"

"We have had almost 40 police search the train at the top of the Buda Hill and here at the terminus," he continued, "and we have found no one. No one could hide or escape from 40 trained policemen. It must be a ghost!"

At that moment the train sounded its bell, ding, ding! Zoltán had seen that all the police were off the train, so he pressed a button to lock the doors and started to drive the train round to the railway shed.

The police dashed to the carriages, but they could not open the doors, although they saw that a few cats still remained on board. They noticed how the points changed by themselves, sending the train towards the shed, and not up the hill. Then they saw the lights of the railway shed go on and its doors open up. When the train had entered, the doors closed. And a few minutes later the lights went off.

"It must be a ghost!" called Gyula to his sergeant.

"A ghost! A ghost!" nodded the policemen round them.

The chief inspector ran over to the railway shed, but the doors were solidly locked. He could not get in, and no one inside could get out. On his radio he called the police station and told them to tell the duty inspector to come round to the station with keys to the railway shed.

The inspector was there within minutes. Police surrounded the shed as the inspector unlocked the doors and put the lights on. A dozen policemen, headed by the chief inspector and the sergeant, streamed in and searched every inch of the shed. But no one could be found, apart from three rather frightened cats.

"Sergeant! I think you may be right," said the chief inspector. "The motor of the middle train is still hot. It must have been up and down the hill. So we were not dreaming. It must be a ghost that drove that train!"

A big cheer went up from the tired policemen, who had been chasing and then searching the cogwheel railway. "A ghost! Hooray!"

Then remembering the remaining cats, the chief inspector called over the sergeant and told him to get on to the Cat Society, so they could take away the cats still on the train to find a home for them.

Afterwards the chief inspector had all nearby households informed that the train had gone up and down hill with no one to be seen at the controls. He concluded that it must be a good ghost, who did not wish to frighten or harm anyone, but who enjoyed driving the train up and down the Buda Hill.

The people living in that part of Budapest were very happy to learn that it was not a criminal or a hooligan driving the cogwheel railway at night, but a good ghost. Many of them put up posters close to the mountain railway, welcoming the ghost train driver. Others went to the end of their garden nearest to the railway, and they gave it a loud cheer as it went up or down during the night. Several planted special flowers or flowering bushes by the railway line to greet the ghost train driver.

Zoltán was very happy to see the posters and hear the cheers, and later to notice the lovely flowering bushes. He occasionally gave an extra ring on the train's bell to acknowledge them, and to let the local people know that there was someone at the controls of the train, even if no one could see him. Ding, ding, ding!

Postscriptum

After a couple of weeks, St Peter thought it was wrong to continue disturbing the people living in the vicinity every night as the cog-wheel railway went up and down the Buda hills. They seemed to be enjoying having the mountain railway driven by a ghost, but for how long?

Rather than wait until they started to complain, he decided to change the railway into a ghost railway at night. It still goes up and down the hill every night, but now it cannot be seen or heard.

And Zoltán still has his reward for having been a good man all his life. He still drives the cogwheel railway up and down the Buda hills every night – but he does not wake people up with the noise of the railway clattering up and down hill and ringing its bell.

But sometimes when the night is quiet, people can still hear a faint ding, ding! as the ghost train goes past. Some, in particular new arrivals in that area, think it is just their imagination. Others know better. They smile, turn over in their beds and carry on sleeping.

- END -